by Johnny Marks
Illustrated by Cathie Shuttleworth

Rudolph the Red-Nosed Reindeer
by Johnny Marks

© 1949 St.Nicholas Music Publishing Co.Inc.USA,
Chappell Music Ltd, London W1Y 3FA

Reproduced by permission of Chappell Music Ltd
and International Music Publications.

Published in Great Britain 1989
by World International Publishing Limited,
An Egmont Company, Egmont House,
PO Box 111, Great Ducie Street, Manchester M60 3BL.
Printed in DDR.

ISBN 7235 8891 0.

A CIP catalogue record of this book is available from the British Library

You know Dasher and Dancer

And Prancer and Vixen

Comet and Cupid and
Donner and Blitzen . . .

But do you re-call
The most famous reindeer of all?

RUDOLPH THE RED-NOSED
REINDEER . . .

Rudolph the red-nosed reindeer
Had a very shiny nose.

And if you ever saw it,
You would even say it glows.

All of the other reindeer
Used to laugh and call him names.

They never let poor Rudolph
Join in any reindeer games.

Then one foggy Christmas Eve
Santa came to say:
"Rudolph with your nose so bright,
Won't you guide my sleigh tonight."

Then how the reindeer loved him
As they shouted out with glee:
"Rudolph the red-nosed reindeer,
You'll go down in history."